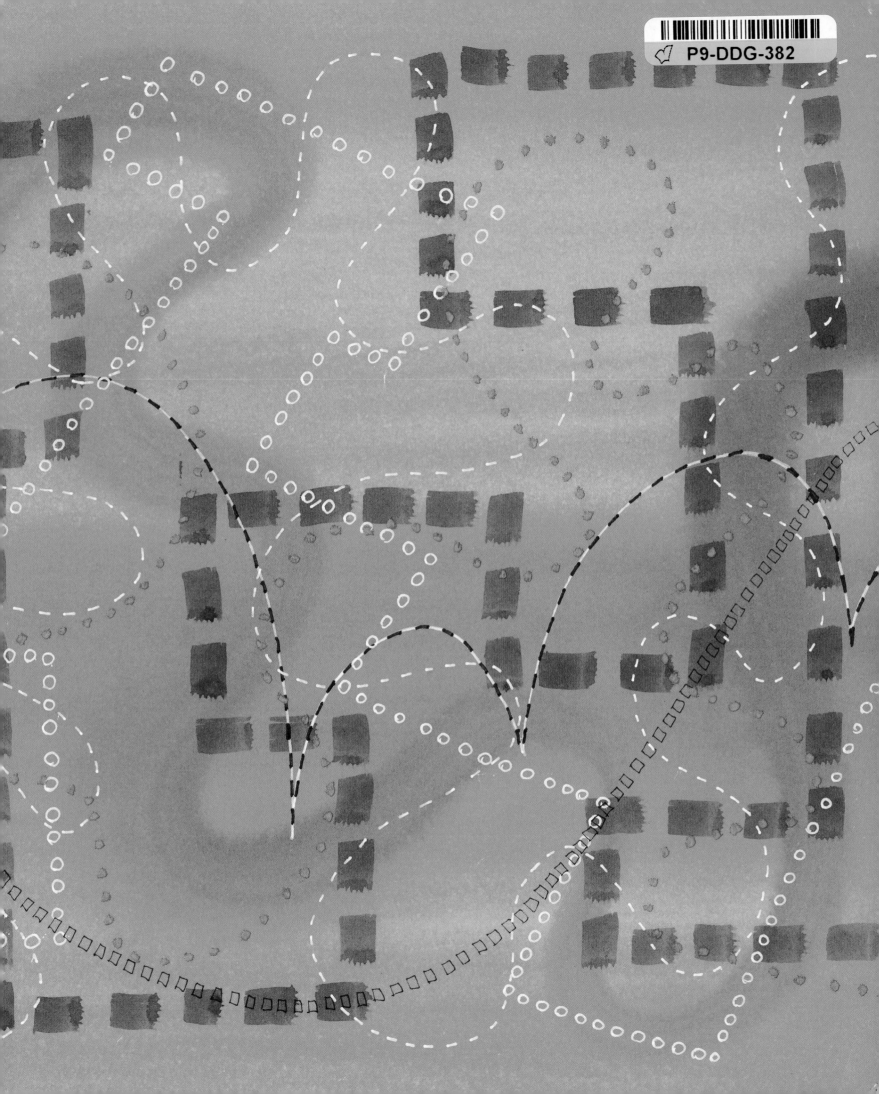

Take an exciting trip through this book! Find the way with your finger. These red arrows on each page show you where to start and where to go next.

For Jan

Translated by Ineke Lenting

Copyright © 2015 by Lemniscaat, Rotterdam, The Netherlands
First published in The Netherlands under the title *Speeltuin*
Text & illustration copyright © 2015 by Mies van Hout
English translation copyright © 2015 by Lemniscaat USA LLC • New York

First published in the United States and Canada in 2016 by Lemniscaat USA LLC • New York
Distributed in the United States by Ingram Publisher Services

Printed in the U.S. by Worzalla Printing, Stevenspoint, WI

First U.S. edition 2016

Library of Congress Cataloging-in-Publication Data
van Hout, Mies
Playground / Mies van Hout; translated by Ineke Lenting
p.; color illustrations; cm.

ISBN 978-1-935954-51-4 (hardcover)

1. Animals—Juvenile fiction. 2. Adventure outdoors.

PZ7 [E]

Playground

MIES VAN HOUT

LEMNISCAAT

Let's go to the playground!

Are you coming?

First, we'll run through the dunes.

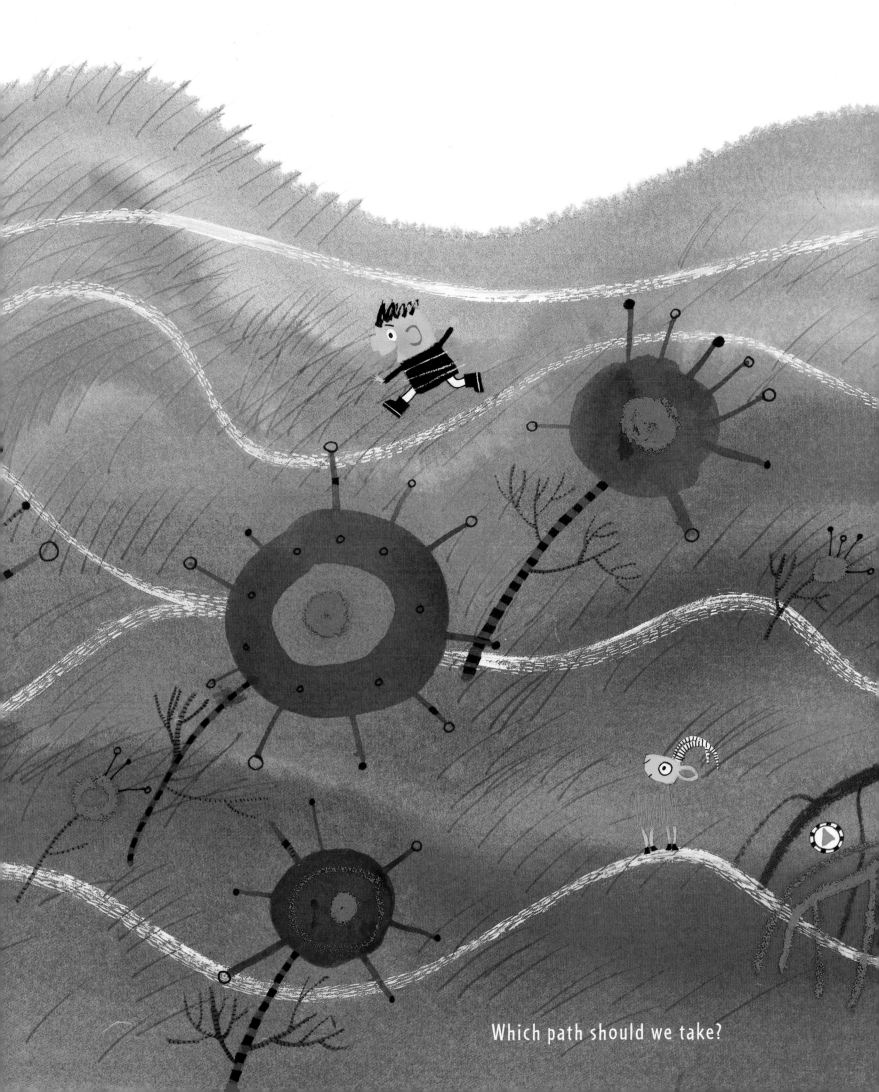

Which path should we take?

We have to climb the trees.

Stay away from the birds' nests—eggs are hatching!

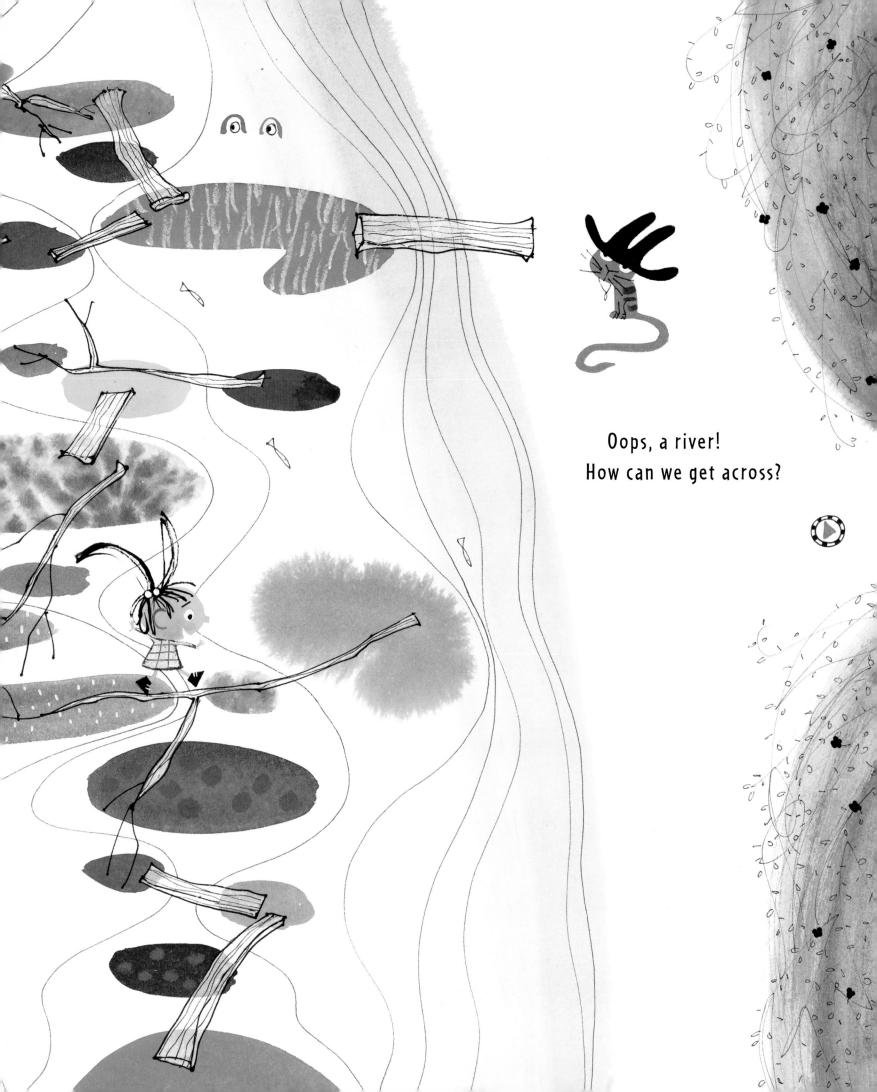

Oops, a river!
How can we get across?

Yummy blackberries!
Let's have a snack
and find the
path again.

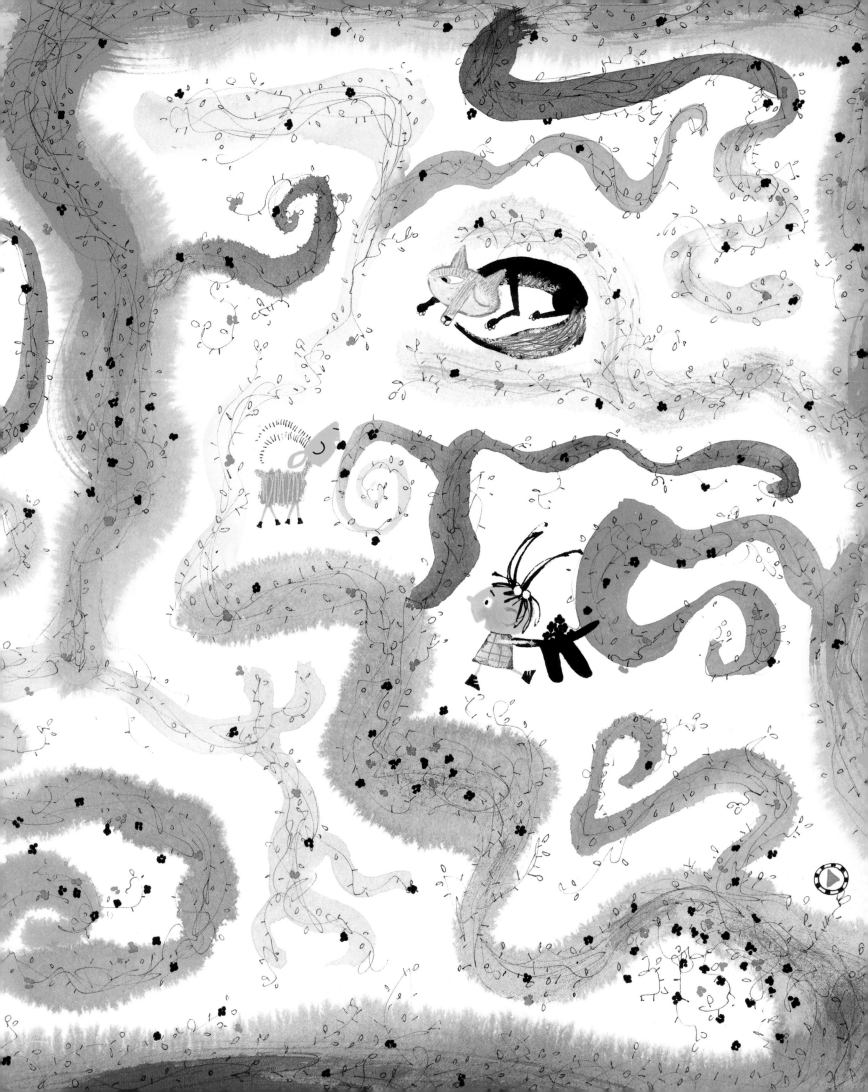

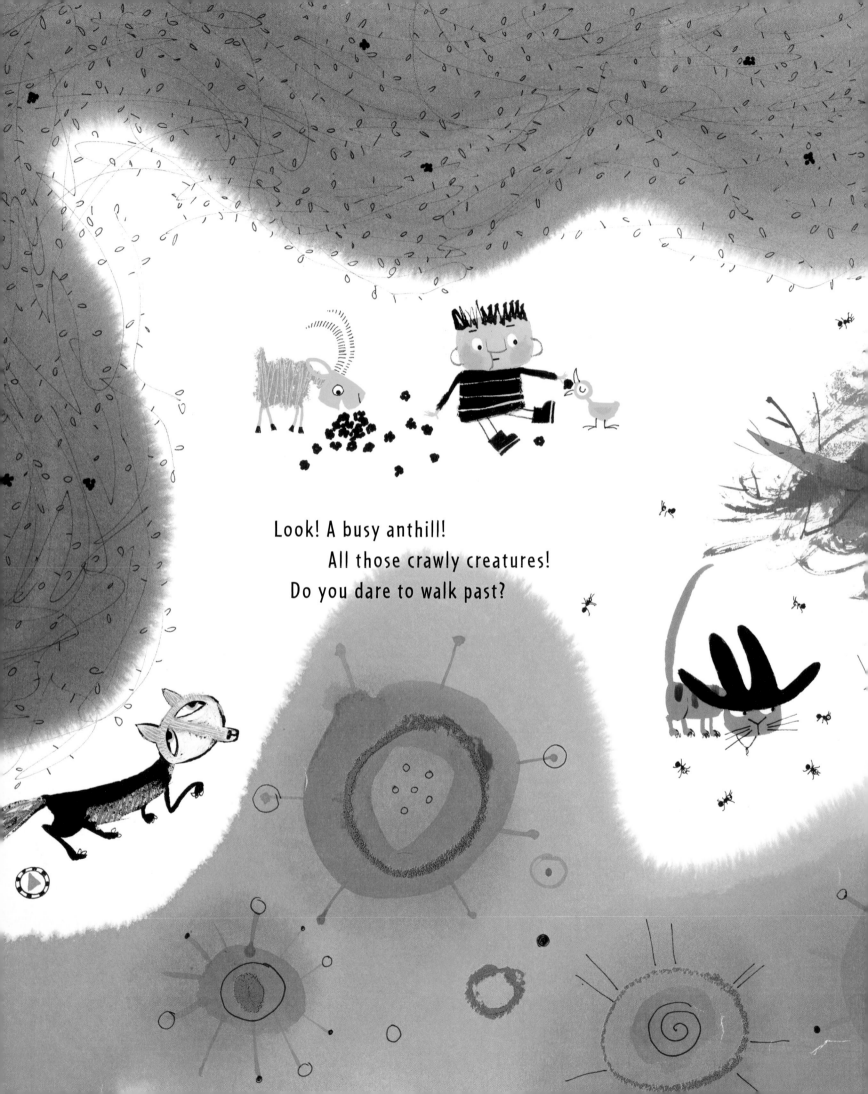

Look! A busy anthill!
All those crawly creatures!
Do you dare to walk past?

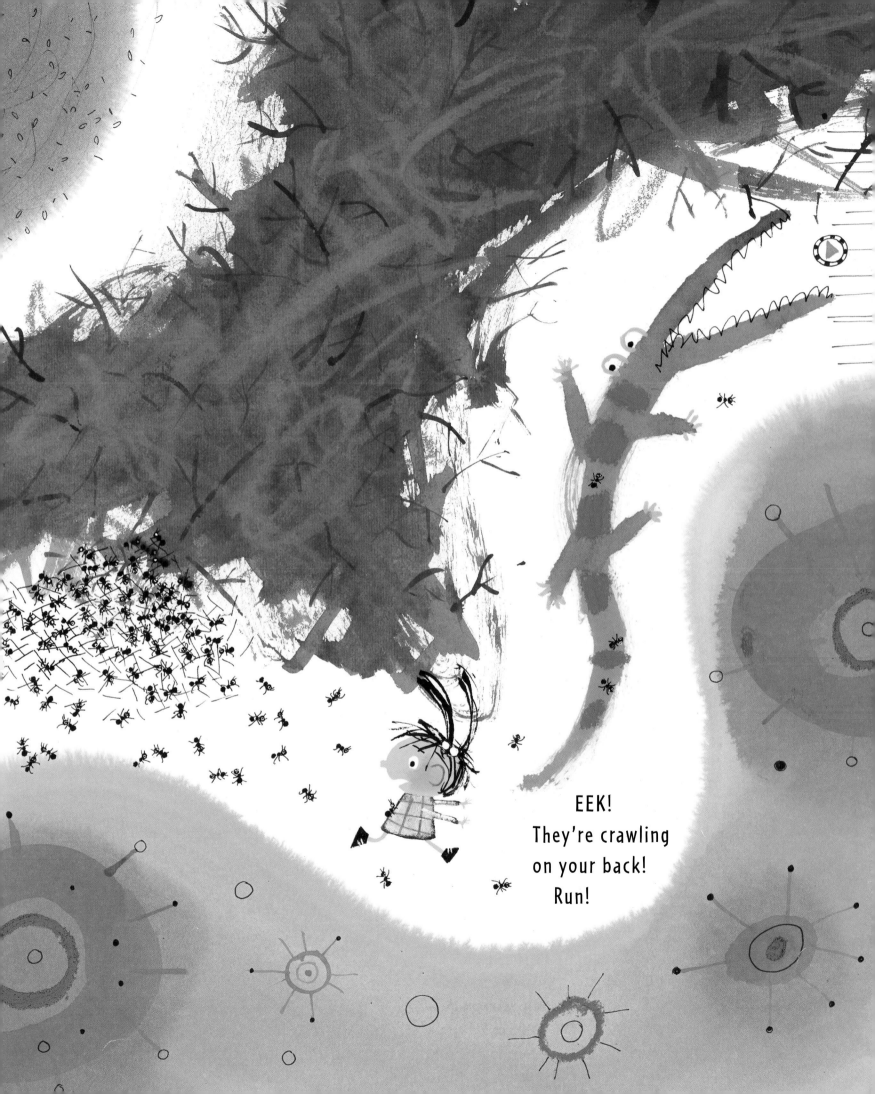

EEK!
They're crawling
on your back!
Run!

Watch out—a cliff!

Let's jump from cloud to cloud.
    That will bring us safely to the mountain.

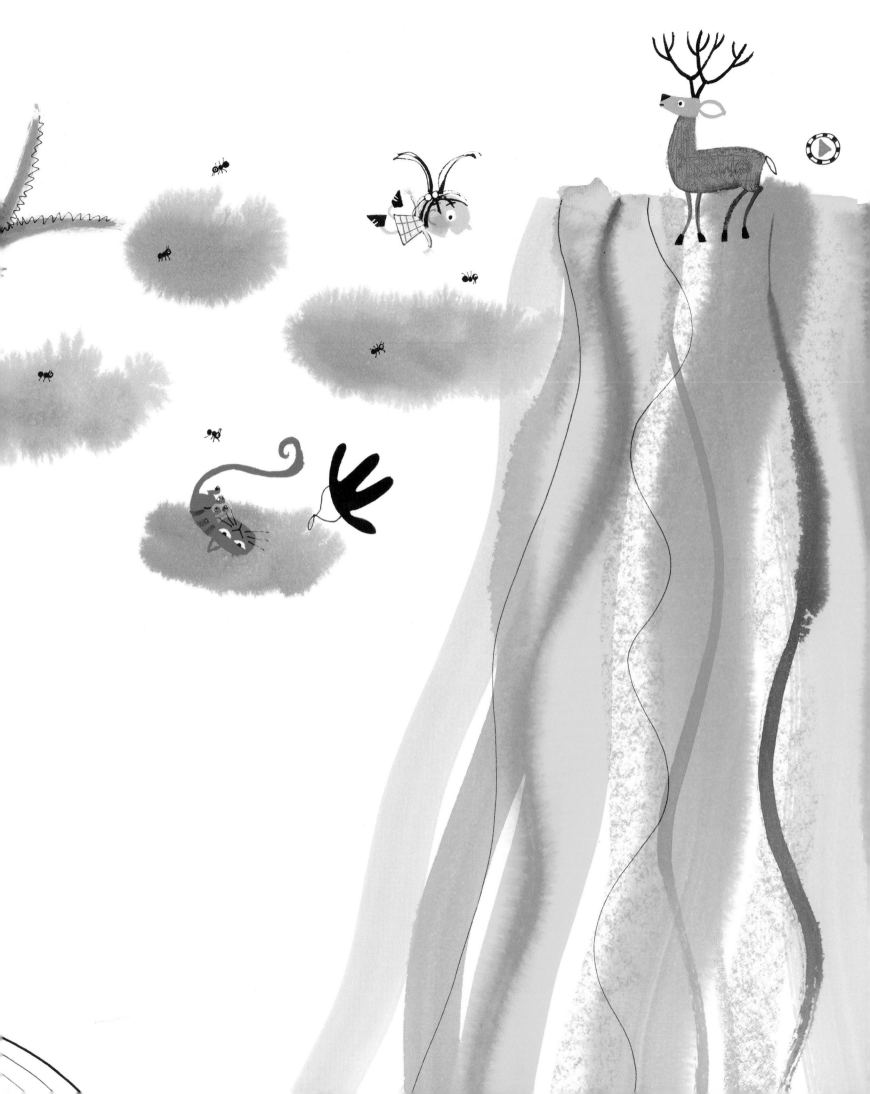

Wheeeee!
It's fun to slide.

We want to do it again!
You too?

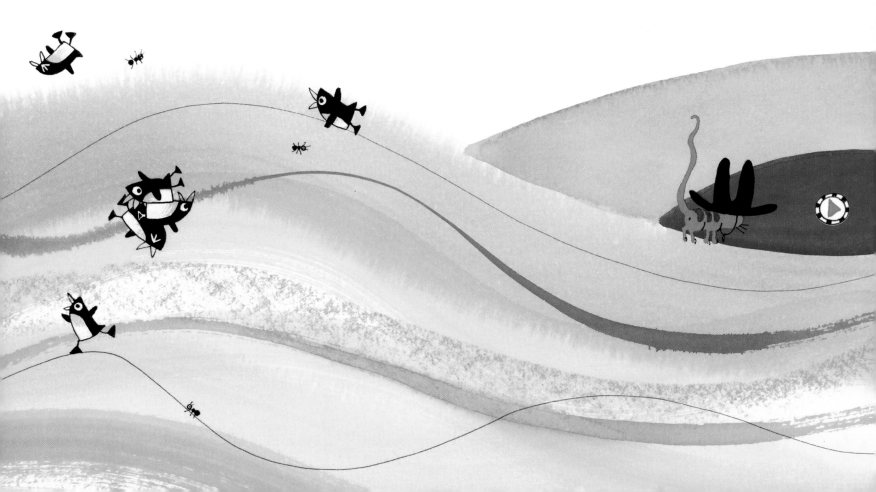

We're almost to the playground.
Just a short trip through the cave.

It's dark in here.
We need to be very quiet
because at the end of the cave—

—lives a huge monster!
Don't wake him up!

Can you step across its legs
without touching them?

There we are!

Let's go back!